The Snowman

The Book of the Film

Raymond Briggs

Pictures from the animated film THE SNOWMAN
selected by Taylor Grant

PUFFIN

PUFFIN BOOKS

Published by the Penguin Group: London, New York, Australia, Canada, India, Ireland, New Zealand and South Africa
Penguin Books Ltd, Registered Offices: 80 Strand, London WC2R 0RL, England

puffinbooks.com
thesnowman.co.uk

First published in Puffin Books 1992
Published in this edition 2008
011-11
Copyright © Snowman Enterprises Ltd 1992
The animated film THE SNOWMAN, produced in 1982, is based on the book *The Snowman* by
Raymond Briggs, first published by Hamish Hamilton in 1978
All rights reserved
The moral right of the author and illustrator has been asserted
Made and printed in China
ISBN 978–0–140–92630–9

Copyright in this recording ℗ Penguin Books 2007
All rights reserved
This edition manufactured and distributed by Penguin Books Ltd 2008

This recording features: "Walking In The Air"
(Composer Howard Blake; Lyricist Howard Blake)
Performer Peter Auty
℗1983 SONY BMG MUSIC ENTERTAINMENT (UK) Limited
Published by Highbridge Music Ltd
Licensed courtesy of SONY BMG MUSIC ENTERTAINMENT (UK) Limited

All rights of the manufacturer and of the owner of the recorded work reserved
Unauthorized public performance, broadcasting and copying of this CD are prohibited

This edition produced for The Book People Ltd, Hall Wood Avenue, Haydock, St Helens, WA11 9UL

When James woke up it was snowing! He got dressed as quickly
as he could and raced downstairs. "Don't forget your boots,"
said Mum. James tugged on his wellingtons by the front door.
He couldn't wait to be out in the wonderful whirling snow.

In the garden James had a brilliant idea: he'd make a snowman!
James rolled a snowball until it was almost up to his waist.
He packed more snow round it until it was as tall as a man.
Then he rolled another snowball for the head. The snowman
shape was perfect, but there was something missing . . .

James rushed into the house. Mum gave him a woolly scarf and a hat, and James found a tangerine for the snowman's nose and lumps of coal for his buttons and his eyes. Then he drew a line for his mouth and the snowman was finished!

By now it was getting dark. "Teatime," Mum called.
James said goodnight to the snowman and went slowly
back indoors.

 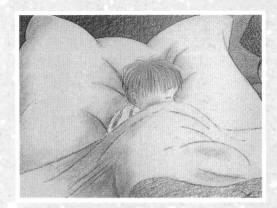 

Then it was time for bed. Mum kissed James goodnight and soon
he was fast asleep.

  When the grandfather clock struck twelve, James suddenly
woke up. He went to the window and looked out at his snowman.
He looked very lonely. James put on his dressing gown and tiptoed
down the stairs.

James opened the front door without a sound.
When he stared out into the moonlit garden he could
hardly believe his eyes – the snowman moved!

He took off his hat politely and bowed. And then he started to walk towards the house. James shook his hand.

"Would you like to come in?" he asked. The snowman nodded.

"We must be very quiet," warned James, "or my parents will wake up."

The snowman sat down in an armchair in the living room
and stroked the cat sleeping by the fire. *Mrreaoowww!*
His hand was freezing! The cat hissed and spat.
The poor snowman nearly fell out of his chair with fright.
James couldn't help laughing.

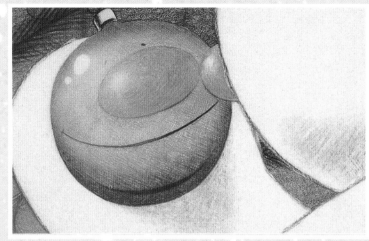

The snowman liked the Christmas tree – he could see his
face in the shiny decorations. But he was too close to the
fire and he had started to melt!

James took him into the kitchen and opened the fridge door.
The snowman looked much happier – until . . .

. . . he turned on a tap. Whoops! Hot water isn't good for snowmen, either!
He soon cheered up when he saw a little snowman on the Christmas cake.
The tiny model looked just like him.

Then the snowman found the fruit bowl and tried some
new noses! He put on a pomegranate . . . a banana . . . even
a pineapple. But the tangerine was still his favourite.

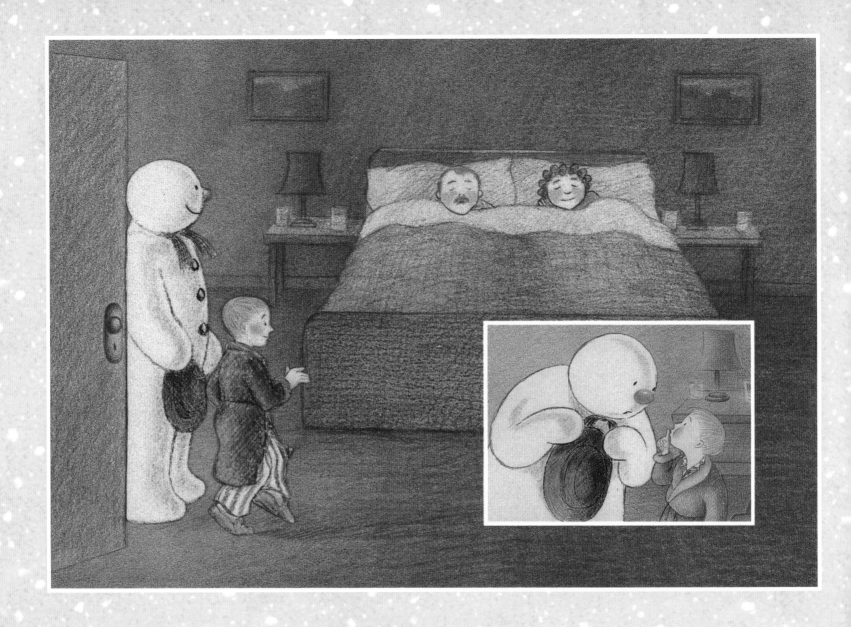

James took the snowman upstairs. "Ssshh! This is Mum and Dad's room," he whispered. The snowman wanted to have a closer look.

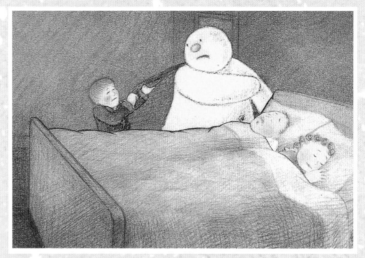

"Careful!" James just stopped the snowman from waking up his parents.

Dad's false teeth were a surprise! The snowman slipped them into his mouth and grinned.

"Let's have a dressing-up game," whispered James.
  The snowman tried out Mum's make-up and her best hat,
put on Dad's trousers and braces, and smoked Dad's pipe.
  "Try some of Mum's perfume," said James.

Oh no! The snowman puffed Mum's perfume spray up his
nose by mistake! He could feel the most enormous sneeze
coming – "Aaaah . . . aaahh . . . aaa-tischoo!"

James took the snowman to his own room. The snowman
found a musical box, wound it up and danced. Oo-oo-ops!
He trod on a roller skate and fell over in a cloud of balloons.
  "Are you all right?" asked James. The snowman nodded.

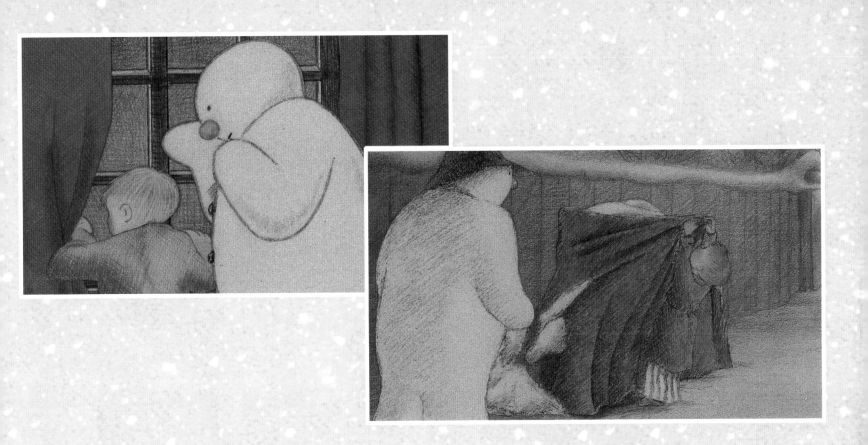

"Come on," said James. "I've another idea.
We can go for a ride!"
  They tiptoed out into the open air to where a dark
tarpaulin covered an old motorbike.

The snowman started the engine and turned on the headlamp.
"I'll hang on tight!" cried James, and the two of them roared off
through the snowy countryside, watched by an owl and some
inquisitive rabbits.

When they came back to the garden, the heat of the engine had made the snowman's legs feel weak. James took him to the freezer in the garage and soon the snowman's legs were as good as new.

As they walked back to the house, the snowman suddenly
stopped. He seemed to have remembered something.
He gripped James's hand and began to run across the garden,
bounding, jumping, leaping, until James found they were flying!

They flew for miles in the icy air. "This way!" cried some of the snowman's friends. Soon they came to the coast and the dark, stormy ocean. A friendly whale waved his tail and blew them a greeting. Then land was in sight again. Where could they be?

All around them was a great forest of pine trees laden
with snow. They landed silently in the icy wilderness.

James could hear music ahead. The snowman pushed aside
some pine branches and led him into a clearing. All the snowmen
in the world had come to a party. There was delicious food and
a band was playing. The snowmen began to dance – with James
in the middle!

James danced with snowmen from all over the world:
from Scotland, Texas, Switzerland, even China!

But his own snowman was best of all. They whirled
and twirled until they were giddy. Look out!
They tumbled over into the powdery snow.
James gave his snowman a big hug.

Guess who else was at the party: Father Christmas!
"I've got something for you, James," he said.
"Come with me."

Father Christmas rummaged among the presents. "This is the one!"
he beamed. It was a beautiful blue scarf.

"Oh, thank you, Father Christmas," said James.

The snowman pointed at the moon sinking over the horizon.
It was time to go.

Once again they flew through the frosty air until they saw
James's house below. Skimming over the hedge, they landed
back in the garden. James hugged the snowman.
"It's been the best Christmas ever," he whispered.
Then he walked back to the house, looking over his
shoulder at the snowman.

The snowman waved goodbye. When James looked out of his
bedroom window he saw him standing in his old place again.
Tired and happy, James fell asleep.

When James woke up he remembered his wonderful adventure.
He rushed downstairs, ran past his parents having breakfast
and opened the door. The sun shone warmly on his face.
But where was his snowman?

An old hat, a scarf, some lumps of coal and a tangerine were
lying on a pile of melted snow. Had it all been a dream?
James felt the soft wool of the scarf in his dressing-gown pocket.
He didn't think so . . .